诚实

善良

谦逊

尊重

Published by Tuttle Publishing, an imprint of
Periplus Editions (HK) Ltd.

www.tuttlepublishing.com

ISBN 978-0-8048-4221-1

Distributed by

North America, Latin America & Europe
Tuttle Publishing
364 Innovation Drive
North Clarendon, VT 05759-9436 U.S.A.
Tel: 1 (802) 773-8930
Fax: 1 (802) 773-6993
info@tuttlepublishing.com
www.tuttlepublishing.com

Japan
Tuttle Publishing
Yaekari Building, 3rd Floor
5-4-12 Osaki
Shinagawa-ku
Tokyo 141 0032
Tel: (81) 3 5437-0171
Fax: (81) 3 5437-0755
sales@tuttle.co.jp
www.tuttle.co.jp

Asia Pacific
Berkeley Books Pte. Ltd.
61 Tai Seng Avenue #02-12
Singapore 534167
Tel: (65) 6280-1330
Fax: (65) 6280-6290
inquiries@periplus.com.sg
www.periplus.com

First edition
16 15 14 13 12   6 5 4 3 2 1   1202TW

Printed in Malaysia

The Tuttle Story: "Books to Span the East and West"

Most people are surprised when they learn that the world's largest publisher of books on Asia had its beginnings in the tiny American state of Vermont. The company's founder, Charles Tuttle, came from a New England family steeped in publishing, and his first love was books—especially old and rare editions.

Tuttle's father was a noted antiquarian dealer in Rutland, Vermont. Young Charles honed his knowledge of the trade working in the family bookstore, and later in the rare books section of Columbia University Library. His passion for beautiful books—old and new—never wavered through his long career as a bookseller and publisher.

After graduating from Harvard, Tuttle enlisted in the military and in 1945 was sent to Tokyo to work on General Douglas MacArthur's staff. He was tasked with helping to revive the Japanese publishing industry, which had been utterly devastated by the war. After his tour of duty was completed, he left the military, married a talented and beautiful singer, Reiko Chiba, and in 1948 began several successful business ventures.

To his astonishment, Tuttle discovered that postwar Tokyo was actually a book-lover's paradise. He befriended dealers in the Kanda district and began supplying rare Japanese editions to American libraries. He also imported American books to sell to the thousands of GIs stationed in Japan. By 1949, Tuttle's business was thriving, and he opened Tokyo's very first English-language bookstore in the Takashimaya Department Store in Ginza, to great success. Two years later, he began publishing books to fulfill the growing interest of foreigners in all things Asian.

Though a westerner, Charles Tuttle was hugely instrumental in bringing knowledge of Japan and Asia to a world hungry for information about the East. By the time of his death in 1993, he had published over 6,000 books on Asian culture, history and art—a legacy honored by Emperor Hirohito in 1983 with the "Order of the Sacred Treasure," the highest honor Japan bestows upon non-Japanese.

The Tuttle company today maintains an active backlist of some 1,500 titles, many of which have been continuously in print since the 1950s and 1960s—a great testament to Charles Tuttle's skill as a publisher. More than 60 years after its founding, Tuttle Publishing is more active today than at any time in its history, still inspired by Charles' core mission—to publish fine books to span the East and West and provide a greater understanding of each.

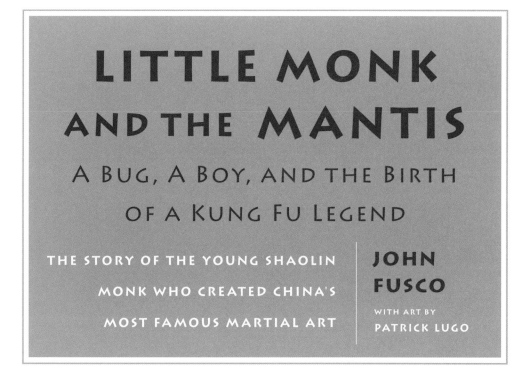

LITTLE MONK
AND THE MANTIS

A BUG, A BOY, AND THE BIRTH
OF A KUNG FU LEGEND

THE STORY OF THE YOUNG SHAOLIN
MONK WHO CREATED CHINA'S
MOST FAMOUS MARTIAL ART

JOHN FUSCO

WITH ART BY
PATRICK LUGO

TUTTLE Publishing

Tokyo | Rutland, Vermont | Singapore

Long ago in Old China, at the foot of Song Mountain, sat a quiet place called the Shao-lin Temple. Shaolin was a monastery where monks lived in peace, tending to gardens and praying by candle and leaving no tracks where they walked. There were student monks, big brothers, uncles, and the master monks—wise old men like Master Feng.

And then there was Wong Long, the small orphan boy who was left on the steps on a long night in the Year of the Monkey.

Wong Long loved his life in Shaolin Temple. He loved lighting the incense for Master Feng; he loved feeding the birds and learning their songs as he walked the mountain trails to gather tea leaf. He even liked sweeping snow from the temple steps. But mostly he loved Kung Fu.

"Kung Fu," said Master Feng, "is a gift from our grandfather monks, an ancient secret that we practice to keep our minds at peace and our bodies strong."

Wong Long knew that his beloved temple had been burned down by bandits and raiders many times in the past. But the monks always forgave the enemy and rebuilt their walls. They did not want to fight, only to defend the child monks and the old ones and the pagodas where they buried the priests. For all life was sacred to a Shaolin monk. Wong Long was taught that the secret ways of Kung Fu were hidden deep in nature. Each monk chose an animal style and studied the ways of that creature so that he might move like it and understand its being and become part of nature as he practiced. This was called the Five Animal styles of Shaolin. It was said that it took half a lifetime to master even one animal.

And so the monks would practice. Practice. Practice. And practice. And when they were done at the end of each day, Master Feng would say, "Practice some more."

Like painting or music, it was beautiful art.

"Kung Fu," said Master Feng, "does not mean fighting. It means accomplishing a skill through hard work over time. A masterful gardener could be said to have good Kung Fu. A flute player who has studied well can have good Kung Fu. So can a cook, or a mother of children, or the man who carves walking sticks."

On the day of the First Plum Flowers of the Spring Wind, Master Feng called Wong Long to the courtyard to observe his martial art. He also summoned Brother Zhu and both young monks bowed deeply to the old master and then to each other, for respect was part of the Kung Fu code.

4

"Some day," said Master Feng, " the Manchus may come again and attack us while we pray or tend to the gardens. We will always ask them to leave and offer them food. But if they do not leave and insist on harming us, we must stand up and defend what is right."

Master Feng sat on the soft earth in the shade of a cypress tree and was quiet for a time. "Show me what you have learned," he said.

Wong Long took his fighting stance. Brother Zhu did the same. It was now time to spar. Brother Zhu moved first. A student of Tiger Style, he held his hands like mighty paws and made his stance rooted yet light. The Tiger style was the way of strength and inner power and Brother Zhu let that force flow through him.

ike a jungle king he whirled and he twirled—He unfurled—TIGER CLAWS!
And when Wong Long tried to strike him he was not there—but behind him! He appeared so big and strong to the littlest monk that fighting back seemed useless. Still, Wong leapt into the air and launched a powerful kick.

But Tiger Way does not defend—One swift attack will bring the end—See him bend—into stripes and tail—or so it seemed to Wong Long who was no longer fighting a student, but a real tiger! What happened next he could not remember. For he was on the ground, looking at the sky, hardly able to breathe.

Brother Zhu, student of the Tiger Style had defeated him. When it was over, the senior brother helped Wong Long to his feet and then bowed to him. Wong Long felt shame, but he returned the honor.

"There is no shame. This is how we learn," said Old Feng. "Brother Zhu has listened to the ancient voice of nature. You must practice more."

"Yes, Master," said Wong Long.

That night, Wong Long sat by the two candles in his tiny room near his sleeping mat. Monks did not keep much, for it was the way of a monk to live spare and not want for things. But Wong Long kept one possession that had belonged to his mother. It was a small and delicate bamboo bird cage that he would sometimes take from the window sill and admire. Sometimes he would imagine the song bird it once held, and he would try to remember his parents before they were lost to the Fever and he was taken in by his uncle. It was whispered that Wong Long had become angry when he lost his parents and he'd become hard to manage. And so his uncle had left him at the Shaolin Temple, hoping that the monks would take pity on a child.

Now Wong Long looked out his window at the night sky and saw the Seven Stars.

When he thought about how many people around the world could see the same stars it made him dizzy. The world was a big place and uncertain. He felt safe high up on the mountain in Shaolin Temple with his brother monks and the kind old masters and the smell of incense and spices.

Yet he felt unworthy. He was too small and did not feel as smart as the other students. He wondered if that was why his uncle left him on the steps and never looked back. He tried hard to learn martial art, but he was always defeated in the matches. What good was he—to anyone?

Sitting in his room and looking at the Seven Stars, he wanted to cry. Instead, he took up his brush and silk, and painted the Chinese characters for the Kung Fu Code:

Respect—To consider yourself and others worthy of high regard.

Honesty—To be truthful.

Kindness—To be gentle and helpful.

Humility—Not to think or consider yourself better than others.

Perseverance—To continue despite opposition, hardship, or discouragement. To never give up.

As he carefully painted each character, he felt his tears disappear like clouds split by the sun.

"Perseverance," he whispered to himself. "I must not give up."

The next day, and for weeks after, the little monk observed Brother Zhu and the Tiger Way. He spent hours in his low stances, developing strong legs and the inner force from deep down in the belly called chi. And when he meditated in the quiet gardens, he thought for hours of Tiger's strong bones but fluid grace and what it teaches a human. "It is like the Yin and the Yang," he heard Master Feng tell Brother Zhu. "The hard turns into the soft, and the soft turns into the hard. There cannot be one without the other just as there can be no light without the darkness before. All things contain their opposite. That is the Yin and Yang."

Soon it felt so good in practice, that he ROARED when he threw his palms out and SCREAMED when he threw his spinning kicks. "I'm King of the Beasts!" he shouted out one day and the senior students chuckled.

He felt ready when Master Feng summoned him to the yard on a chilly morning. Waiting there was Brother Ming, as tall and willowy as bamboo. He and the smaller monk bowed deeply to Master Feng and then to each other.

"Please," the old master said softly. "Show me what you have learned."

The students took their fighting stances. Wong Long stared into Brother Ming's calm eyes. He drew a breath into his lower belly. Then he struck! Like a tiger he whirled and twirled and curled his fingers into tiger claws and struck with powerful palm like thunder.

But Brother Ming was not there. He was already behind Wong, standing on one leg with his arms outstretched like wings and one hand pinched into the shape of a fierce beak. The Crane style was the way of essence and grace and Brother Ming flew into the air. Like wings his arms flapped—They struck and they trapped—Wong Long's punching fist, right by the skinny wrist. Elegant Crane in flight. And the next thing he knew, he was face down in the flow- ers. But tigers do not quit. He rolled over and did a leg sweep, trying to trip the Crane Style monk. Brother Ming lifted his leg softly, spun, and struck with a thundering wing—or so it seemed—and little Wong Long was upside down with his head in the fish pond.

He heard people laughing, but when he shook the water from his ears, he realized it was only the sound of birds in the banyan trees and his own inner voice. Still, he blushed.

Master Feng used his wooden staff to lift himself. When the young brothers bowed to him, he returned the respect. "Brother Ming has listened well to nature," he said. "You, Wong Long, must practice more."

"Yes, Master," said the little monk.

The snows came to Honan Province.

This was a time when the sap stopped flowing in trees, and so the monks followed nature and slowed down their practices. They spent more time inside, seated in meditation or memorizing the ancient books. But not Wong Long.

Master Feng watched out the window as the boy practiced Kung Fu in the snow. His soft boots barely left tracks as he practiced Dancing Crane over and over, always trying not to think too much about the movement, for Kung Fu, like painting must flow freely and cannot be forced.

The next day, Master Feng went to the window and saw that Wong Long had spent the entire night standing on one leg like a Crane. On his bald head was four inches of new snow. Master Feng smiled then brought hot tea out to the monk.

"Perhaps I am ready," said Wong Long, still standing like a Crane. "Perhaps I am ready to spar with my senior brother who has mastered Snake."

And so, on the last day of winter, the little monk was called to the courtyard to battle Brother Jin, a student of the mysterious Snake Style.

Little Wong leapt on light feet, spinning and dipping his wings like an elegant Crane.

But Brother Jin became as Snake—soft, but alive with inner force—Like swimming on lake—The mystery of Snake—Wrapped in a coil—With two hands to foil—Every attack—Snake strikes then draws back!

And Wong Long found himself in the snow. "Maybe Crane is not for me," he told Master Feng. "Practice," said the kind old man.

In Spring the first plum flowers returned and Wong Long practiced even harder. He sparred against the boy who studied Leopard Style, only to lose by a fist. For Leopard is the way of speed—strong like Tiger, but faster. Wong Long did excellent Snake, but he could hardly see the blazing strikes of his opponent.

In Summer heat, Wong Long faced a master of the Dragon Style—the one that teaches spirit and majesty. Twisting, turning, rising, falling—the Dragon student was the toughest of all. Wong Long decided to try everything against him—Tiger, Leopard, Snake, and Crane, and even a style called the Long Fist—yet he could never touch the proud Dragon who seemed to ride the wind as he sent the little monk flying high. When it was done they bowed lowly to each other.

"You have fought each animal style," said Master Feng as he walked with Wong Long along the garden path. "What have you learned?"

"I have learned that I am always defeated," said Wong Long. "I have learned that there is always someone better than me. Even with all of my practice."

"Have you truly listened to nature?" asked the old master.

As Wong Long stopped to consider this, Master Feng walked on in silence. Wong Long looked back toward the courtyard to see his brother monks practicing the Five Animals and Kung Fu sword and stick.

"Practice more and you will find your Kung Fu," he heard Master Feng say from somewhere in the flowers.

"Yes, Master," little Wong said. But what he really meant was "No, Master. I am done practicing."

That night, while the temple slept in silence and candles flickered in the pagodas, Wong Long packed his only possession: the little bamboo bird cage. He tightened the leather straps on his boots and gathered his robes about himself. Before he put out the last candle in his room he took up his brush and painted one Chinese character on the wall. It was the character that meant good-bye.

He looked out at the Seven Stars of a summer night, far out over the mysterious lands beyond the temple. His heart pounded as he made his decision.

Wong Long ran away.

When the sun came up over Song Mountain it turned the land the color of saffron spice. Wong Long awakened beneath a pine tree. He had slept huddled in his robes, hoping that no beasts would scent him and find him. The mountains of China were full of tigers and leopards, snakes and wolves. Sometimes bandits wandered up Big Angel Gully, looking for monks to rob. But what could they take from a little monk except for a bamboo bird cage that held no song?

It was only the darkness that had frightened him, but he remembered Master Feng's teachings about the Yin and Yang, and how there can be no darkness without light—so he knew that the sun would rise again. And as it did, it warmed the earth and he felt relieved to be away from the temple and such perfect students. He had run far from his defeat and his weakness and he felt better for it. Yet, he missed his room and the gardens, and the kind voice of Master Feng. He missed the morning chants and the smell of incense. Why couldn't he win just one match? Even by luck. The Shaolin monks were famous for their Kung Fu. He did not deserve to be among them.

As he sat in the hillside grass he felt a sadness like he had never known. Maybe there could be no happiness without a little sadness, he thought. Because without some sadness once in a while, how could one ever know what happiness really is?

But now he was not even sure which way he should run, which mountain pass he should follow. Wong Long lay himself down in the grass and cried. He cried until the crickets went silent. And then his ears heard something nearby, a faint sound. It was in the grass not far from his head. A praying mantis, as small and delicate as a dried leaf, sat perched on a blade of grass, his hands folded as if in humble prayer. But something was coming toward it through the grass: a large, hard-shelled beetle, its antennae pointed forward. It made a rustling sound in the fallen pine needles.

Wong Long watched, both curious and worried.

He did not want to see the praying mantis eaten up by the bully, but he did not want to be bitten either, so he remained where he sat. The mantis meanwhile rested motionless on the blade of grass so human-like with hands together in silent prayer. The beetle did not even slow his approach as he bulled his way through the grass and used his many legs to pull the praying mantis down and prepare to eat it. But when he attacked, the praying mantis caught the beetle's legs in his claws and pulled him off balance. Wong Long watched, amazed, as the beetle attacked again, but the praying mantis locked his legs in his powerful forearms and at the same time he moved aside and used the large beetle's own weight against itself, flipping it over onto its back.

The beetle was angry and turned itself to attack again. Now the two insects were locked in combat and Wong Long knew that the smaller one could not last. But the praying mantis again used its claws to hook and strike, and now it climbed up the beetle striking quickly and repeatedly and finally grabbing its antennae and pulling it over on its back once more.

This time the beetle righted itself, looked back at the praying mantis, and scurried away. Wong Long watched the little mantis return to its quiet prayer in the grass. "Praying Mantis," he whispered. "Perhaps you have much to teach me."

Wong Long picked up a little stick and got onto his belly to study the insect. Gently he poked at it. The praying mantis remained very still, then suddenly trapped the stick in his clawed forearms and Wong Long could not move it. The little monk smiled for the first time in days.

"I shall name you," he said to the tiny creature. "I shall name you...Teacher."

Wong Long gently placed the praying mantis in the little bamboo cage and began to study his movements. What a wondrous creature Nature had made—none other quite like it. Wong Long stood up in the grass and mimicked the way that it moved, bending his elbows inward and curling his hands into praying mantis claws. He mimicked the way his little Teacher stood still as a way to bluff, then suddenly hooked and captured a strike, faster than a snake could dart its tongue.

For months he observed the ways of Praying Mantis, sometimes letting him out of the cage to go his own way and live amongst nature. Wong Long crawled on his belly behind him, watching everything the tiny mantis did. Once it encountered another praying mantis and Wong Long watched a spectacular match between the two, claws locking claws, until Teacher won the bout. "What a Kung Fu master you are!" Wong Long said.

Wong Long put Teacher back in the little bamboo cage and carried him down into Big Angel Gully to a clearing where the sun was warm. Removing his robe, Wong Long stood in a praying mantis stance and practiced the movements. For hours he practiced. But when he turned back to get his robe, it was gone.

"What has become of my robe, Teacher?" Wong Long said, searching the banks of the stream. But teacher just perched inside the bamboo cage as if in gentle prayer.

Just then, a crazy chattering broke the silence.

High in a tree a monkey danced on branches. In his hands was Wong Long's robe. "Monkey!" shouted the shirtless and skinny Wong Long. "Forgive me, but you have no use for a robe! Please return it at once!"

But Monkey shimmied to a higher branch, teasing and chattering and trying to put the golden robe on over his monkey head. Wong Long climbed the tree and gave chase. But Monkey dropped out of the branches and flopped about on the ground, one arm stuck in the robes.

Wong Long dropped from the tree and rolled in the dirt. He lunged for Monkey, but the little ape ducked low and scrambled backward and sideways and then spun away making a sound like laughter. "Naughty Monkey!" shouted Wong Long, "I will catch you yet."

But Monkey could not be caught. His feet moved in riddles that Wong Long could not solve, and after a while Wong Long began to laugh at himself. He was tired and he sat down near the little bamboo cage, watching Monkey run about with the stolen robe.

"He is little, but he is tricky, do you agree, Teacher?" Wong Long said to the silent mantis. "If only I could be so tricky with my feet...while using your praying mantis hands."

Wong Long leapt to his boots in excitement. "How quick are you, Monkey?" he yelled as he set chase again, this time following the tracks in the dirt and tracing the tricky footwork. As he did so, he held his hands like praying mantis and boxed with his own shadow.

Monkey dropped the robe under a tree and ran away.

"Today is a wonderful day, Teacher," Wong Long said to Praying Mantis. He leapt onto a river rock and struck a Kung Fu stance that was his own. He remained very still, the silence of the forest all around him. On the rock ledge behind him, his shadow looked just like a praying mantis.

"I am listening," he said.

23

Wong Long did not know how many days had passed, but the leaves had turned colors and the hollows of Song Mountain held blue mist at dawn . He knew it was time. And so, carrying Praying Mantis in the small bamboo cage, he journeyed back to the pine tree where he had first found the wise little one. Kneeling in the grass, he opened the cage and waited for the praying mantis to leave. But his teacher remained with his hands folded in prayer. So Wong Long did the same.

He prayed for many things, but mostly, he prayed in thanks for what nature had taught him. After a long while, the mantis slowly left the cage and perched himself on a blade of grass.

"Thank you, Teacher," the little monk said. "I will never forget you."

He bowed to the praying mantis, and as he walked away, it seemed that Praying Mantis was bowing to him.

Master Feng was lighting candles inside the Hall of Ancestors when he heard a commotion outside. Calmly, he walked out into the yard and what he saw brought tears to his eyes.

The littlest monk had come back. He had been gone so long that his hair grew in like little pine needles. The senior brothers walked alongside him, asking him where he had gone and why, and telling of how they missed him.

"I missed all of you, too," he said.

Then he looked up and saw Master Feng standing there with his staff. The kind old man looked like a grandfather who thought he had lost his grandson forever. He hugged the little monk.

"What did you do for so long in the high mountains?" Master Feng said.

Wong Long thought for a moment and then said, "I practiced."

Master Feng stared at him for a long moment. Then he smiled.

The next day, the monks of Shaolin Temple were up before the sun. They chanted and prayed, and then walked in single-file silence to the courtyard to do their eighteen exercises for body and mind. Master Feng took his favorite seat on the ground beneath his beloved cypress tree.

"Brother Zhu," he called. "And Brother Wong. Please."

All of the monks gathered to watch as Brother Zhu and Wong Long walked to the center of the courtyard. They knew why they were called, and so they faced each other respectfully.

"Show me what you have learned," said the master.

Wong Long bowed to Brother Zhu who did the same. And then the senior monk took the fighting stance of the Tiger. His muscles had become even stronger since Wong Long was away and when he slowly drew his arms back, he seemed to change into a powerful jungle cat. He had been practicing Tiger Style even harder now, and many of the monks covered their eyes as they watched him circle the little Wong Long. Then he struck!

Like a fierce Tiger he clawed at his opponent. But Wong Long stepped aside at the same time that he grabbed Brother Zhu's wrist and let Tiger's own strength carry him into the garden. A great hush fell over the temple courtyard as everyone looked on.

27

Brother Zhu rose from the dirt and seemed surprised. Wong Long was in a fighting stance that no one had ever seen before, not even Master Feng. The little monk had his weight back on his rear foot as he held his hands up like a praying mantis, waiting very still for the next attack.

Brother Zhu charged.

Wong Long stepped out on his heel then spun on tricky feet, moving like Monkey. Praying Mantis catching fist—Tiger caught now by the wrist—Like Mantis pulling in his prey—Then sending Tiger on his way! Right into the fish pond. "I cannot believe what I am seeing," whispered Master Feng.

Brother Ming was called up next. Like elegant Crane he stood on one leg and spread his graceful wings. But Wong Long met every move like Praying Mantis taught him, and he shuffled his feet like naughty Monkey, and in no time at all, the student of the Crane was upside down over the wall.

Now the monks were all standing, silent and astounded. Next, Wong Long defeated Snake. Then he defeated the blazing fast Leopard. Finally, he did battle with the Dragon, and to everyone's amazement, he stood victorious while the majestic Dragon rode the wind—right into the fish pond.

Nobody moved for a time. Then Master Feng stood with the help of his stick and approached the little monk. "Someone has listened well to nature," he said. "For one thousand years our Shaolin Temple has stood tall on the Five Animal Styles of Kung Fu. Now you have returned here with a strange style of your own that has defeated all. What have you named this style?"

Wong Long had not thought about naming what he had learned. But now he stood there feeling like he had something to share, like he was worthy. Like he had finally found his Kung Fu. "It is called Praying Mantis, Master. Seven Star Praying Mantis."

"Seven Star?" said the old master, curious.

"Yes, Master. For I wish it to spread to as many people as can look up and see the Seven Stars at night."

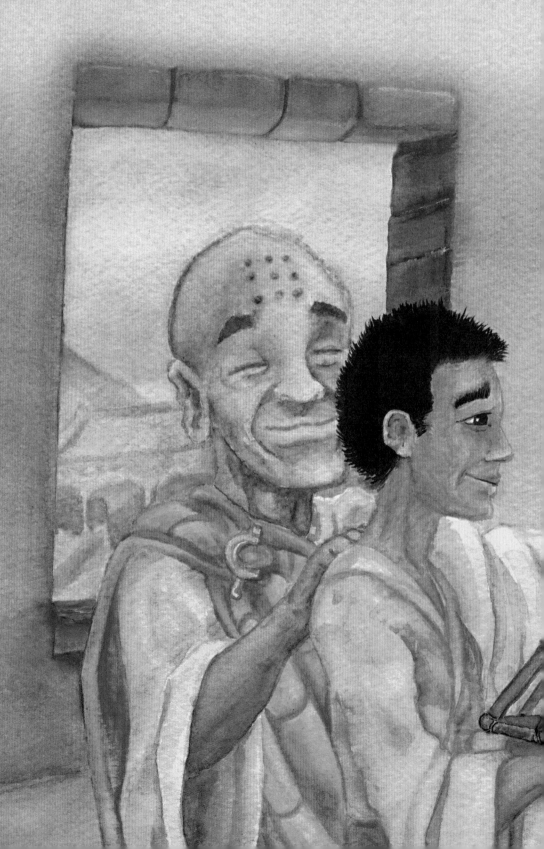

Wong Long bowed to the old master, and the master bowed back. He was proud of the littlest monk. As Wong Long started across the courtyard, Brother Zhu followed him. "Please, little brother," he said. "Teach me this Praying Mantis."

Soon all of the Shaolin monks were around him, asking the same.

That night, when Wong Long returned to his room, he was tired, but happier than he had ever been. Two candles were lit by his small sleeping mat, and on the wall between their soft flame, someone had touched the brush and painted Chinese characters.

It was the characters that meant "welcome home."

歡
回

迎
家

AUTHOR'S NOTE

The story of Wong Long is obscure Chinese history that has become martial arts legend.

Wong Long (Wang Lang) lived and studied at the Shaolin Temple in Honan Province during the late Ming Dynasty (17th Century) where he became founder and master of the Praying Mantis style of Kung Fu. He grew up to be a patriot, defending China from an emperor who wished to destroy the temples and have more control over the common people.

Praying Mantis Kung Fu continues on today and is practiced all around the world. It is recognized as one of the true treasures of China's martial arts.